THE NILE FILES

Stories about Ancient Egypt

THE CRAFTY CROCODILE

by Philip Wooderson

Illustrations by Andy Hammond

FRANKLIN WATTS

First published in 2001 by Franklin Watts
96 Leonard Street, London EC2A 4XD

Text © Philip Wooderson 2001
Illustrations © Andy Hammond 2001

The right of Philip Wooderson to be identified as
the Author of this Work has been asserted by
him in accordance with the Copyright, Designs
and Patents Act, 1988

Editor: Lesley Bilton
Designer: Jason Anscomb
Consultant: Dr Anne Millard, BA Hons, Dip Ed, PhD

A CIP catalogue record for this book
is available from the British Library

ISBN 0 7496 4190 8 (hbk)
0 7496 4371 4 (pbk)

Dewey Classification 932

Printed in Great Britain

CONTENTS

NOTICE

Welcome to the Shrine of Sobek,
the Crocodile God

His son, Klaptrap, lurks in the river.
He feasts on human bods.
You might be next, so do not dither.
Bring gifts to lower the odds.

Brill

Keeper of
the Shrine
Bogflatt
Egypt

4

CHAPTER 1
A DEATH IN THE FAMILY

"We've had our adventures," said Dad. "We've had our ups and downs, but sometimes I can't help thinking that it would make a nice change to let someone else do the work."

"If you could just pay us some wages," mumbled one of the crewmen, heaving hard on the oar.

"As soon as I've traded these mud bricks," said Dad. "Though come to think of it, lads, these bricks might come in useful to build my retirement villa."

"'Scuse me!" A man on another boat passing the other way was waving to get their attention. "I'm looking for someone called Dipstick."

The lads guffawed, "What a name!"

Dad looked a bit sheepish. "Who's asking?"

"I bring him an urgent scroll. It's from his brother's widow in Bogflatt."

"My brother hasn't got any widows!" Dad seized the scroll. "Where's my scribe?"

Stupor opened one eye. "Did I dweam it, or ith your name wierlly Dip-thtik?"

"Just read this, quick!" Dad demanded.

Stupor took his time. "Ith bad newth about your bwuvvah."

Dad's jaw sagged. "Nubb? What's happened?"

"Been killed by a cwoc."

"Killed by a crocodile! Don't be stupid. Nubb's always been so . . . careful."

"Not this time," said the boatman. "The crocodile swallowed him whole. Only thing it spat out was a sandal. Not much left for mummification."

But Dad didn't seem to be listening. Instead he stared at Ptoni. "With Nubb gone, the farm will be mine."

"But what about Uncle Nubb's wife, Dad?"

"Krumpet?" Dad frowned. "What about her?"

"Well, won't it belong to her now?"*

"The poor girl," said Dad. "She's no farmer. But not a bad looker. I wonder if she might . . ." His frown gave way to a dreamy smile. "Perhaps I should do my duty and take her under my wing."

* Egyptian women could inherit property – see page 60.

It took several days to sail all the way up the river to Bogflatt. Dad's family had been farmers there for longer than they could remember.

Dad pointed across to the far bank. "Just look at that swanky new shrine. I've never seen that before."

Ptoni thought it looked a bit tacky. But Bogflatt looked even more tacky.

All the houses were built out of mud bricks, and the jetty was crowded with clapped-out boats loading up with even *more* mud bricks.

Dad aimed their boat for the rushes. As soon as the keel hit the bank, he jumped out into the mud. He had to steady himself by clutching a handy signpost.

"Thikk!" exclaimed Dad. "I remember young Thikk – he was a bit of a bully, but I soon sorted him out. And look at him now."

Dad pointed at the squat, ugly man on the jetty who was waving wildly. "What a warm friendly welcome!"

"Get out of the water, you fool!" cried Thikk. "Do you want the croc to get you?"

Dad puffed up the steps to the jetty. "The same croc that guzzled my brother? I'd have thought you'd have caught it by now."

"Catch Klaptrap? Where would we be then? No-one would bring us any offerings –"

"Shhhhh!" A man in a leopard-skin cape gave Thikk a hard dig. "Thikk only means Klaptrap's holy, because he's the son of Sobek, the crocodile god.* So – hold on, don't I know you?" His fishy eyes boggled. "Dipstick!"

* Find out more about Sobek on page 61.

"Yes," cried Dad. "And you're Thikk's weedy brother. So why are you dressed like a priest, Brill?"

"Brill's in charge of the shrine," said Thikk. "But what are you doing with bricks on your boat? *I* make all the bricks around here."

Dad told them the bricks had been his reward, for sorting out Pharaoh's obelisk. "But that was before I heard the Sad News."

"Yes, poor old Nubb," said Brill. "I still haven't charged his widow for all the burial costs."

"What was there to bury?" asked Ptoni.

Thikk cleared his throat. "It's the thought that counts."

"Indeed," agreed Brill. "You must give thanks – with a gift to the god Sobek at my shrine."

"Give thanks? What for?" asked Ptoni.

"It's a very great honour that Klaptrap chose your uncle," said Brill. "Though if he thought Nubb tasted yummy, he might get a taste for your family – so you'd better look where you're going."

"He lurks," said Thikk. "He's so patient. He strikes when you least expect it."

"Who strikes?" asked Stupor. "Thikk's bwuvvah?"

"Oh dear," Dad shook his head sagely. "Old Stupor's not going to last long. Klaptrap's sure to get him."

CHAPTER 3
HOME SWEET HOME

Walking along the riverside path was very scary indeed. Even Ptiddles, the ship's cat, was jumpy. Every fallen tree trunk and mud bank looked like a lurking crocodile. And by the time they got to Nubb's farm, the sun was low in the sky, casting long black shadows in the most frightening places.

"We just have to be careful," said Dad in a low voice.

"You said Nubb was careful," said Ptoni, looking round the neat farmyard.

"Hello! Can anyone hear me? I've come home at last!" called Dad.

There were rattles and clunks from the far side of the yard, and a girl climbed out of a cage, slamming the door behind her. Inside the cage was a baboon.

"Krumpet!" cried Dad. "But you look so . . . young! Let me offer you brotherly help."

"I'm not –"

"Young? Never mind. We're as young as we feel, aren't we, Krumpet?"

"Who's that?" shouted someone else from inside the house. "Who are you chatting up now, Fidget?"

"Fidget?" gasped Dad. "Nubb's *daughter*? The last time I saw you, Fidget, you were a teeny baby –"

A woman appeared at the farmhouse door. She looked a bit like Fidget, except she was twice the size, with straggly grey hair and a wrinkly face that sagged as she noticed Dad.

"Dipstick," she said. "You've missed the funeral, but I suppose you'd better come in."

The house was small but comfy, and there was a good smell of cooking.

Dad eyed a big tray full of cakes. "May I? It's good to be home. I'll manage the farm, don't you worry."

"You won't. I like farming," said Krumpet. "It's Fidget I'm worried about."

"Just find her a nice young man," said Dad, taking the largest cake.

"Nubb found her one," said Krumpet.

Fidget snorted loudly. "Not a very young one, and he's not very nice."

"But he's quite well off," said her mother. "And you agreed to the marriage. That's why Nubb made all the arrangements."

"I hadn't met anyone else then."

Dad straightened his back. "You've met someone else?"

Fidget sighed, "Yes. A *real* man."

"That wretched Hunk," said Krumpet.
"One of Lord Lumpit's bodyguards. He passed
by on a hunting trip. All muscle, no brain.
Now he's gone back to Thebes, so why can't
she just forget him?"

"He left me his pet baboon."

"The dratted brute!" cried her mother. "It
eats its head off. Oh, Dipstick, Fidget must
think of her future. If she backs out of this
wedding, no other man in Bogflatt will ever
want to marry her. It's your duty as her uncle
to try to make her see sense."

Dad reached for another cake. "Well, Nubb was always so careful. If he arranged this marriage before he got chomped by that Klaptrap," he took a big bite from the cake, "he must have been sure things would work out with this first husband-to-be. Who is the chap? Is he local?"

"Thikk? He makes bricks," said Krumpet.

Fidget stalked out of the room.

"B-b-but–" Dad was spitting out crumbs of cake, "isn't Thikk married already?"

"He was. Klaptrap ate his wife."

"But Thikk's old and ugly," said Ptoni.

"Good looks aren't everything," Dad said, glancing at Krumpet. "And Fidget can't hope to do better, Ptoni. Not in a place like Bogflatt. I mean," Dad turned back to Krumpet, "she can't really think this Hunk would settle for country life when he can be in a big city like Thebes, chasing other young –"

Knock. Knock.

"That'll be Thikk now," said Krumpet.

While she went off to fetch Fidget, Dad gave Thikk a warm welcome, patting him hard on the back. "I soon got the girl to see sense. You'll make a happy couple. And seeing as we'll be brothers, why don't I lend you a brotherly hand helping you to run your business?"

"What, shifting my bricks?" asked Thikk.

"I'm talking about the shrine," Dad winked.

"Brill's shrine's doing fine," grinned Thikk. "He thinks I should use Fidget's dowry to build a new inn for his pilgrims."

"But that'll cost a small fortune. How much did Nubb save?" Dad wondered.

"More than enough," said Thikk. "And very sensible of Nubb, too. Money makes a girl much more attractive. You're lucky you haven't got daughters."

Dad shot a quick glance at Ptoni. "I'll drink to that."

Thikk chuckled. "I'll fetch us some wine."

"He's a man of the world," said Dad. "And thanks to him and his brother, Bogflatt's starting to prosper. In fact, when they get all those pilgrims coming to stay at their inn, they're going to need a ferry to get them to the shrine. Why shouldn't it be *Hefijuti*? The lads can be crewmen. I'll get you to flog the tickets, and Stupor can do the refreshments."

"While you take it easy. But where will we live? I don't think Krumpet wants us here."

"Oh, she'll just work in the fields and do our housekeeping, Ptoni. I'll find a young wife with a dowry. I bet Fidget's got a few nice pretty friends."

"What's that about a dowry?" asked Krumpet, returning without Fidget.

"I was just saying," smirked Dad, as Thikk started pouring the wine, "that if Nubb hadn't had the good sense to save up a dowry for Fidget, I'd have been happy to fork out. It's all in the family, Krumpet."

But as they were raising their goblets, there was a yell and a crash, and a series of slithering bumps.

"Has Fidget fallen downstairs?" gasped Ptoni.

Krumpet reached the door first – in time to see an intruder beating it out of the house.

Ptoni and Dad gave chase, but the man vanished into the darkness. And when they got back to the house, they found Krumpet up in her chamber, peering into an empty chest. "The family treasure's been stolen!"

Thikk peered over her shoulder. "You mean my dowry's gone missing – with only two days till the wedding?"

"We could call it off," murmured Fidget.

"You can't back out now," thundered Thikk. "The whole of Bogflatt will despise you."

"So what do you think we should do?" wondered Dad.

"Just find the treasure," growled Thikk. "Or you're going to have to fork out like you promised, remember?"

FOR SALE

CHAPTER 4
THE MYSTERY THICKENS

They didn't sleep much that night, stretched out on the hot flat roof.

Dad kept tossing and turning, mumbling about the lost dowry, while Ptoni stared up at the stars, thinking about his poor cousin having to marry old Thikk.

When dawn broke at last, he sat up. "We're not going to find Aunty Krumpet's treasure unless we can catch the thief, Dad."

"I was just nodding off," grumbled Dad, rolling over and going to sleep.

So Ptoni set off by himself, running as fast as he could, just in case Klaptrap was lying in wait. But he made it. He got to Bogflatt in time to find the first traders setting up stalls in the market place.

He helped an old woman unloading her vegetables and told her about the break-in at Krumpet's.

"There's only one thief in this village, and that's young Kreep," said the woman.

"Where does he live?"

"With me. I'm his old Ma," said the woman. "But you won't find him at home now. The poor boy's just been arrested. You'd do better to ask that guard over there."

The guard was standing outside a mud shack. He wouldn't let Ptoni in. So Ptoni peered through the window. A man was sitting on the ground with his head in his hands.

"Kreep," Ptoni called, "was it you who broke into Krumpet's house last night?"

"Of course. I'm the village thief. But there was nothing to steal."

"What? Everything's gone from her treasure chest!"

"Bad luck. I wouldn't be sitting here now if I'd got my hands on her loot. But I've got a Ma to support so I tried my luck at the shrine. That's where I got nabbed. Now I'm for it. Brill's going to feed me to Klaptrap."

When Ptoni got back to the farm he found Dad out in the yard and passed on his news about the village thief.

"That's odd," said Dad. "I've been checking the house while Krumpet was out in the fields and the treasure's not here either. So where else could it be?"

Ptoni looked at the cage. Hunk's pet baboon was squatting on his box. The sun was shining into his eyes, so they gleamed like golden nuggets.

Dad stiffened. "I've got an idea."

So had Ptoni. He was thinking that Fidget hadn't made much of a fuss about the loss of her dowry. It was as if it hadn't surprised her.

As if . . . ?

Ptoni stared at the box in the baboon's cage . . .

"I bet it was Nubb who took the dowry," said Dad.

Ptoni let out his breath. "Before the crocodile got him?"

Dad gave a nasty laugh. "Old Nubb was always too careful to let any crocodile get him. More likely he did a flit."

"Why d'you think he did that, Dad?" asked Ptoni.

"Hah! He wouldn't have wanted to give all his treasure to Thikk."

"He could have just cancelled the wedding."

"Then he'd have been saddled with Fidget."

"Except . . ." Ptoni moved away from the cage and Dad strolled after him grinning. "I don't think Thikk would want her, not without any dowry."

"That's true." Dad thought for a moment. Then his eyes nearly popped from his head. He turned round and stared at the baboon's cage.

Ptoni feared that he had given the game away.

But Dad had other ideas. "Nubb must have reckoned that *I'd* pay Fidget's dowry. That's why he got Krumpet to send me that urgent scroll."

"You can't think Krumpet's involved?" asked Ptoni.

"Why not?" blustered Dad. "She's a shrewd old bird. She'll know where Nubb's holed up. I bet he's having a great time in Thebes. But I'm not going to let them outsmart *me*."

"So what are we going to do, Dad?"

"We'd better tell the bad news to Thikk and Brill. They won't be building their new inn now."

Dad hurried along the river bank, pushing through the rushes without looking to left or right. Ptoni warned him he ought to be careful. "That crocodile might be lurking."

"I bet you he doesn't exist," breezed Dad stepping over a fallen tree trunk.

Ptoni wasn't so sure.

When they got to the jetty they found it crowded with locals. The guard was holding on tight to Kreep. He was wriggling, sniffling and pleading.

"Oh, spare me, please. For my Ma's sake!"

"You should have thought of her," snarled Brill, "before you broke into my shrine."

"But that's why I did it."

"So push off!"

Kreep went in with a great splash.

Then Thikk turned to Dad, "Found my dowry?"

"Bad luck," said Dad. "Nubb took it and he's probably spent it now. I wish I knew where he'd gone."

"Gone to the Other World, stupid, where Kreep will be joining him shortly."

"I can't see the crocodile," said Ptoni, watching Kreep who was swimming towards the far shore.

"We have to be patient," said Brill.

"We didn't have to wait long for Nubb," said Thikk. "That croc was ready and waiting for him."

"It got my goat," said a woman. "And then it got my husband."

But Kreep waded out of the water and went hobbling off up the bank. The crowd hissed and booed.

Brill raised his hand. "Klaptrap has shown rare mercy." He turned to Kreep's Ma. "So you must all give thanks by taking a gift to the shrine. And as for you," he nodded to Dad, "the god Sobek will expect you to do your duty."

"What duty?"

"You've got to do as you promised, and fork out for Fidget's dowry."

Dad gawped. "But I won't! Er . . . I mean, I can't!"

"Yes, you can. You've got that big boat," said Thikk.

"Not anymore he hasn't," said Brill, rubbing his hands. "It's moored at the jetty here and we're going to keep it in place of the treasure. We'll use it to ferry the pilgrims across to my new inn. Dipstick can work as a crewman."

Going home Dad was ranting. "I can't be one of their crewmen. The lads will laugh in my face. But what am I going to do?"

"Watch where you're treading," warned Ptoni.

"Brill and Thikk are a pair of thieves," Dad moaned. Then he stopped in his tracks and slapped his forehead. "*They* must have stolen the treasure, before Kreep crept on the scene."

"They *might* have," Ptoni admitted. "But Dad," he had to be honest, "I don't think –"

"Who cares what you think? I'll search their shrine," Dad blustered.

"You can't. It's against the law, Dad. If we're caught we'll be buried alive in sand."

"There won't be anyone guarding it now. Come on, let's borrow a boat."

By the time they found a small boat the sun was going down. And by the time they reached the shrine, it was so horribly dark they couldn't see where they were wading as they climbed out of the rushes. But Dad didn't care. He was jaunty – even when he shone his lamp on the notice outside the shrine.

Dad managed to force the door.

The entrance hall was badly built, with bulging brick walls and a sagging roof. It was crowded with frightening statues. "You stay here on guard," Dad decided, "and I'll go and pick up our treasure."

His footsteps echoed away.

Ptoni waited a long time. He heard water slopping outside, and then a raw rattling sound as something pushed through the rushes, and then a slow dragging sound. He shivered. He thought of Klaptrap. The noise got louder and nearer. The back of his neck went prickly.

"Dad," he whispered.

No answer.

Bump. Bump.

Too late to get out now. Whatever it was blocked the entrance. His heart was thumping. He panicked. He ran deeper into the shrine. He found himself in a big cave. All around him were flickering oil lamps, more statues and offerings to Sobek.

But where was Dad?

He listened again, only to hear that same noise – of something smooth but heavy shifting across the flagstones.

He hollered, but his voice was hoarse. "Hey, Dad, there's something out there!"

Dad scrambled from under the offering table looking quite pleased.

"Well spotted, Ptoni. I couldn't find anything here."

43

Then his eyes nearly popped from his head.

"But what's behind you?"

A huge shadow was sliding over the wall – of a monster with open jaws. There was no doubt about it.

"Klaptrap!" yelled Dad.

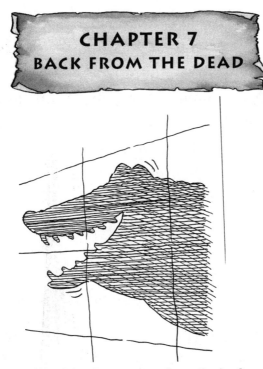

The crocodile hit the ground at their feet. It looked huge. It was wrapped in bandages!*

And the man who had carried it into the shrine stood back and laughed."Like my mummy? But I'll be blowed – it's Dipstick! What are you doing in here?"

Dad stared at the man in amazement. "I could ask the same question, Nubb. I thought you'd gone to Thebes."

---

* All kinds of animals were mummified – see page 62.

Nubb gave Dad a brotherly hug. "I've just come back from there."

"Why?"

"Lord Lumpit brought me. I'd better explain it all."

So Nubb told them his story. On the day the crocodile got him, he had been talking to Thikk. "I told him the wedding was cancelled, because Fidget didn't want him, now that

she'd met someone younger. So Thikk pushed me in the river and the crocodile grabbed my foot. It dragged me under the water, but I was a lucky man." He showed them his bandaged foot. "My sandal came off and I broke free. When I came to the surface, Lord Lumpit's galley was going by. I grabbed a steering oar. And as I was being hauled out, Hunk managed to spear the brute."

He kicked the mummified reptile. "It won't catch anyone else now."

"So now you're back in Bogflatt," said Dad.

"Yes, what a relief," said Nubb. "Lord Lumpit took me to Thebes because I needed help from his doctor. But now that I'm better, he's brought me home. Along with some guards and Judge Talon."

"What does *he* want?" Dad looked worried.

"Thikk pushed me in the river, so the Judge thinks it's more than likely Thikk gave his wife the push as well. And Brill's in *very* big trouble."

"What for?"

"Pretending to be a priest and running a phoney shrine without Pharaoh's seal of approval. He'll be buried alive in sand," said Nubb.

"So everything's turning out fine," grinned Dad. "Except you've lost your treasure. Though that won't matter so much now, if Fidget's not going to get married."

"Of course she's getting married. That's why Hunk's at the farm now. And that's why I've come to the shrine. I reckon Brill swiped my treasure."

Dad chuckled. "So did we. But we've had a look and it's not here."

"Where else could it be?"

"Don't ask me, Nubb."

"He hasn't a clue," said Ptoni, "but I think I know who has. You'd do better to ask Fidget."

Yes, Fidget knew Thikk wouldn't marry her
without a dowry. So she hid the treasure in the
box in the cage. But when she showed it to
Hunk, he didn't seem all that bothered.

"It's not the money I want. It's Fidget.
She's so lovely. But if you insist, Nubb, then
half will do."

The wedding took place the next day.

Lord Lumpit came to the feast.

51

And so did the lads, Dad and Ptoni. Ptiddles enjoyed heaps of roast meats and Stupor raised his goblet (over and over again) to drink to the Happy Couple.

Then Nubb made a kindly speech, hoping that Dad and Ptoni would think of the farm as their home, which made Krumpet squawk with dismay.

"Perhaps we will," said Dad. "Ptoni's spent his whole life on the river. You'd be amazed if I told you all our adventures . . ."

He told them.

". . . though on the other hand," Dad rolled on, "I've still got to think of my crewmen."

"They could help on the farm," offered Nubb.

"But what about Ptiddles?" said Ptoni. "He wouldn't be happy on dry land."

"Nor me. I'm a trader at heart," said Dad. "I'm taking those mud bricks to Thebes."

"Why go all the way to Thebes?" asked Nubb.

"That's Uncle Dipstick's wedding present to us – a lift to Thebes," said Fidget.

So when the feast was finished they all walked back to the boat. The lads helped Stupor to stagger on board.

Dad followed.

And Ptoni.

And Ptiddles.

"I wish I was going," said Kreep, watching them raise the sail. "I'd do very nicely in Thebes, Ma, with all those tombs and rich palaces."

"Nubb's still got some treasure," whispered his Ma.

"And we've got each other, dear Krumpet," said Nubb.

"And Klaptrap's mummy," said Krumpet, as the boat pulled away from the river bank.

But as Stupor made himself comfy underneath the spare sail, he got a bad shock.

"It's a cwoc. Help!"

"A croc on board?" yelled the lads. "Jump over the side!"

"You fools," scoffed Dad. "It can't hurt you. It's only that mummified croc. I'm going to sell it in Thebes, lads, as a collector's item."

"But chief, it belongs to your brother," said one of the lads.

Dad waggled his shoulders. "I . . . er . . . took it. So I can pay you your wages."

"Oh Dad."

"Oh Dipstick!" chorused the lads.

"Though on the other hand," Dad carried on, "if it fetches the price I'm expecting, I might buy a new boat instead."

"You wouldn't get rid of this old crock?" protested a lad, giving the mast a fond slap.

"Why not?" asked Fidget. "A smart boat would be nice. What will you call your new craft, uncle?"

"*The Young Cwoc*?" mumbled Stupor.

"*The Spirit of Klaptrap*?" said Ptoni.

"Never!" Dad was outraged. "That is an insult to Sobek! I shall call my new craft . . ." a sudden smile lit up his face, "The *Crafty* Crocodile!"

Women and Marriage

Egyptian women had a lot of freedom. They could inherit and own property and make their own wills. Some girls married very young, at 12 or 13. A newly-married couple owned everything jointly. If a man divorced his wife, she had the right to keep any valuables that she had contributed to the marriage. Women could also divorce men.

Sobek

The Egyptians believed that a special animal or bird was chosen by each god as a container for his spirit when he visited earth. The god Sobek chose a crocodile as his sacred animal. Sobek was god of the water and also represented Pharaoh's might. As the crocodile could strike quickly,  snatching and destroying its prey, so Pharaoh could strike, destroying his enemies and wrongdoers. Sobek had temples honouring him throughout Egypt.

Mummified Animals

An animal specially chosen by a god to house his spirit on earth was kept in a temple and treated with great honour. When the animal died (of natural causes), it was mummified and buried like royalty. Egyptians believed that all animals had a little bit of divine spirit in them. So when they died, people sometimes had

them mummified before burial, hoping to win the god's approval. Remains have been found of mummified falcons, cats, dogs, snakes, mongeese, crocodiles, baboons and even beetles. In one set of galleries, deep under the desert, millions of mummified ibises (birds sacred to the god Thoth) were discovered lined up in rows in pottery jars.

Join Ptoni and his Dad up the Nile
in these other books.

THE SCRUNCHY SCARAB
0 7496 3649 1 (Hbk)   0 7496 3653 X (Pbk)

The town of Feruka is having a big celebration, but all Dad has to
sell are some dried-up figs and a few old flasks of oil. Fortunately
Ptoni finds a lucky scarab beetle – so perhaps things will change.

THE MISSING MUMMY
0 7496 3650 X (Hbk)   0 7496 3654 6 (Pbk)

Dad goes to collect some wine he is owed by Slosh, the merchant.
But poor Slosh has died, and someone has stolen his mummy.
It's up to Ptoni to find it, and to claim the wine.

THE FEARFUL PHARAOH
0 7496 3651 3 (Hbk)   0 7496 3655 6 (Pbk)

Pharaoh Armenlegup is having a big festival to celebrate his long
reign. So everybody is happy – everybody, that is, except Dad.
He's been sentenced to death!

THE HELPFUL HIEROGLYPH
0 7496 3652 1 (Hbk)   0 7496 3656 4 (Pbk)

Pharaoh has ordered Dad to pick up some taxes for him – but Dad
can't read. So he hires an old scribe to teach Ptoni how to
understand the hieroglyphs. It's a harder job than they thought!

THE JINXED SPHINX
0 7496 3987 3 (Hbk)   0 7496 4021 9 (Pbk)

Ptoni and Dad only have a damaged sphinx to trade in the market
place. But when three dancing girls hitch a lift on their boat, things
start to look up.

THE POINTLESS PYRAMID
0 7496 3988 1 (Hbk)   0 7496 4022 7 (Pbk)

When three sinister-looking men ask for a lift, Dad is happy to
oblige. But trouble breaks out even before they reach their
destination – the spooky Pointless Pyramid!

THE WOBBLY OBELISK
0 7496 4189 4 (Hbk)   0 7496 4370 6 (Pbk)

An obelisk is to be erected in honour of Pharaoh Armenlegup in
the courtyard of the Temple at Hokus. Dad is put in charge of the
work gang. But the obelisk begins to wobble . . .